Architecture

Clothing and Fashion

Culinary Arts

Dance

Decorative Arts

Drawing and Painting

Festivals

Sculpture

THE WORLD ART TOUR
Decorative Arts

By Sandy Mitchell Pavick

MASON CREST
Philadelphia • Miami

Mason Crest
450 Parkway Drive, Suite D
Broomall, PA 19008
(866) MCP-BOOK (toll free)
www.masoncrest.com

Copyright © 2020 by Mason Crest, an imprint of National Highlights, Inc. All rights reserved. No part of this publication may be reproduced or transmitted in any form or by any means, electronic or mechanical, including photocopying, recording, taping, or any information storage and retrieval system, without permission in writing from the publisher.

Printed in the United States of America

First printing
9 8 7 6 5 4 3 2 1

Series ISBN: 978-1-4222-4283-4
Hardcover ISBN: 978-1-4222-4288-9
E-book ISBN: 978-1-4222-7535-1

Cataloging-in-Publication Data is available on file
at the Library of Congress.

Developed and Produced by Print Matters Productions, Inc.
(www.printmattersinc.com)

Cover and Interior Design by Tom Carling, Carling Design, Inc.

CONTENTS

Introduction 6
   Key Terms 8
1 Africa 9
2 Asia 21
3 Europe 33
4 Latin America and the Caribbean 45
5 Middle East 57
6 North America 69
7 Oceania 81
   Further Reading & Internet Resources 94
   Index 95
   Author's Biography & Credits 96

INTRODUCTION

Decorative arts—the furniture, housewares, and ornamentation that people use in the places where they live—can tell you a lot about a culture and what its people hold most dear. This volume looks at cultures, design styles, and trends around the globe, from ancient times to the present.

Decorative art, as opposed to fine art, has a purpose outside of simply being beautiful. It can be furniture, pottery, tools, blankets, items to use in religious services, or glasses and vases, to name just a few examples. It can be primitive or elaborately adorned, large or tiny, heavy or lightweight, expensive or affordable. The only thing that decorative art is not, is ordinary.

Decorative art involves more than just creating useful items that are both attractive and functional. It offers us a peek into the history, the raw materials available, and the tools used by a particular culture. Some decorative art forms remain today; others, such as the majority of the silver objects crafted by the Inca, have been lost to history. Some have become iconic, such as Grecian urns or Chinese ceramics; others offer commentary on current events of the day, such as the mid-twentieth-century *Sputnik* light fixtures.

As we explore the many different types of decorative art from six continents, we'll track the evolution of skills like wood carving and metalsmithing as civilizations became more advanced. We'll see the influence of religion and war on the type of decorative art objects a society creates. We'll also identify the leading pioneers in different decorative art movements, from ancient Egypt to contemporary America. We invite you to join us on this journey. One thing we'll guarantee: You'll never look at your sofa, mixing bowl, silverware, or rugs the same way again.

Facing page (clockwise from top left): Jade lion from Vietnam; Australian aboriginal didgeridoos; Peruvian textiles; tilework at the Shah Mosque in Iran; Art Nouveau subway entrance in Paris, France; Barcelona chairs by Ludwig Mies van de Rohe and Lilly Reich.

KEY TERMS

Bakelite: The first type of plastic to be commercially manufactured, Bakelite was patented in 1909. It was used in a variety of decorative arts applications, from early telephone sets to cabinet hardware to kitchenware. Bakelite items are highly collectible today.

Bas-relief: A French term that describes adornment to a panel or piece of furniture that seems to "grow" a three-dimensional motif or design off a flat surface on the back.

Calligraphy: The decorative art of writing.

Embroidery: The art of decorating a piece of fabric with thread or yard using a needle.

Enamel: Made by fusing glass to another material.

Etching: The process of using acid to "cut" a design into a piece of metal or glass.

Finial: A decorative adornment at the top of a furniture piece, lamp, or other object. Finials are decorative rather than functional.

Gilding: A technique of applying a very thin layer of gold to the surface of wood, porcelain, metal, or stone.

Inlay: A technique used in decorative arts where one material is set into another to form a pattern or other adornment. Inlay is commonly used on hardwood parquet flooring, in classic musical instruments, and in high-end automobiles.

Lacquer: Any of a variety of clear or colored synthetic organic coatings that typically dry to form a glossy finish.

Mandala: A sacred Hindu and Buddhist decorative art form that symbolizes the universe. Mandalas are generally round and are the central element to most home shrines.

Minimalism: A modern American decorative art movement that reduces the elements in a room to the bare essentials and the materials used in a piece to strictly what is needed for its function.

Mosaic: A piece of art made by assembling very small, glazed, flat ceramic tiles to form a pattern or image.

Motif: A distinctive and often recurring feature in a design or design style.

Mural: A large painting applied directly to a wall or ceiling.

Neoclassicism: The revival of elements of Greco-Roman design, such as scrolls, columns, gilded surfaces, and finials.

Opaque: Something that is impenetrable to light.

Palette (as it related to decorative arts): The range of colors used in a design scheme or in a single object.

Plywood: A board made with thin layers of wood that have been heated, glued, and pressed tightly together by a machine.

Porcelain: A ceramic material made by heating clay and other materials in a kiln to temperatures between 1,200 and 1,400 degrees Fahrenheit. Porcelain is stronger, tougher, and more translucent than most other types of ceramics.

Rococo: A style of decorative art popular in Europe, particularly France, in the 1700s, marked by lavish ornamentation.

Sculpture: Any type of three-dimensional art, in materials such as stone, wood, clay, and so on.

Textiles: A broad term that includes any type of woven fabric. In fact, "textile" comes from the Latin word *textus*, which means "woven."

Translucent: Able to have light pass through.

Victorian: A decorative arts movement that roughly corresponds to the reign of England's Victoria I (1837–1901). This era coincided with the advent of mass-produced furniture and other decorative art pieces, thus making such items affordable to the middle class. Victorian style is notable for its somewhat overly furnished rooms, elaborately carved furniture, collections on display, and patterned wallpaper.

CHAPTER 1 AFRICA

The continent of Africa spans 11.7 billion square miles, contains 54 countries, and is home to more than 1.2 billion people (16 percent of the world's population). In addition, most of the continent was colonized during the nineteenth and early twentieth centuries. These British, German, French, Belgian, and Portuguese settlers brought their cultures with them and left their distinct marks on African decorative arts. Decorative art in Africa is a mélange of tribal design, colonial influence, and modern style.

COLONIAL FURNITURE AND DECOR: A BLEND OF STYLES

The nineteenth century brought a rush of adventure-seeking Europeans to Africa, following in the footsteps of eighteenth-century explorers and traders such as Henry Stanley, David Livingstone, and Richard Burton. For around 100 years, Great Britain ruled places like present-day Kenya, Nigeria, and Sudan; the French occupied today's Algeria, Morocco, and Sierra Leone; the Belgians claimed the Congo; the Portuguese set up camp in Mozambique; and the Germans took over Tanzania. Only Liberia and Ethiopia remained African-ruled.

British colonial décor was a reflection of colonists adapting to their environment. Mosquito netting could be found around the bed, and white cotton upholstery was often displayed.

Ratan furniture, similar in style to this chair, was used by British colonists.

    The European soldiers, farmers, adventure-seekers, and administrators all brought their best furniture, tableware, and decorative items to the "Dark Continent" and adapted these designs to their new climate and the materials at hand. The result was a colonial design style that favored furniture made of hardwoods like mahogany and teak, which wouldn't rot in the humid equatorial climate.

    British colonial décor featured many "camp," or campaign-style, pieces. These chairs, desks, and tables with brass hardware could be easily disassembled, folded, and carried with their owners as they moved to a new property, set up camp during a safari, or took to the road on a military campaign during the Boer Wars. The colonists also kept their steamer trunks nearby, using them as coffee tables or for storage at the foot of their beds. Along with these European elements, colonists incorporated native elements such as animal hides and pelts. They also adapted to their environment by using things like mosquito netting, khaki and white cotton upholstery, and rattan furniture.

AFRICAN TEXTILES TELL A STORY

Arguably, the most noteworthy of the many African decorative arts are the textiles that come from the continent. More than just a way to create fabric, weaving in many African tribal cultures was and is a way to celebrate life and create a bond among families. Some of the oldest surviving examples of woven cloth have been found in Africa, in archaeological sites in Burkina Faso and Nigeria. Textiles have traditionally been used in Africa to tell stories and record historic events.

Of course, because Africa is so vast and has been inhabited by so many different people, a variety of unique types of African textiles can be found. Some of the more notable include the following:

- <u>Akwete</u> (a unique handwoven cloth, using hemp, raffia, and cotton) and *ukara* (cotton stamped with *nsibidi* symbols), from the Igbo people of present-day Nigeria
- *Adire* (tie-dyed cotton) and *asa oke* (heavy, hand-loomed fabric) from the Yoruba people of present-day Nigeria

Kente cloth is produced on a loom. It is striped interwoven silk and cotton cloth.

A woman wears a shweshwe dress.

- Kente cloth (striped interwoven silk and cotton cloth), from the Ashanti and Ewe people of present-day Ghana
- Bark cloth, from the Buganda people of present-day Uganda
- Mud cloth (made using fermented mud) from the Bambara people of West Africa
- *Kanga* (colorful, lightweight cotton) and *kitenge* cloth from the lake region near present-day Tanzania
- *Shweshwe* (a printed cotton cloth) from today's South Africa
- *Ankara* (animal wax prints) from West Africa

For Africans, today as well as in the past, textiles offer a sense of context and identity. When people from different parts of the continent meet one another, the fabric they are wearing tells others where they are from and to what tribe they and their ancestors belong.

EGYPTIAN DECORATIVE ART: GODS AND GOLD

Egyptian decorative art is distinctly different from that of the rest of Africa. More Middle Eastern than African, Egypt's civilization dates back to the fourth century BCE. Ancient Egypt is notable for its many elaborate palaces and tombs, most of which were decorated with gilded statues, intricately cut stones, and ornaments with cut gemstones. Egyptians pioneered many of the design and architectural elements that are still used today. In addition, they were among the first to use and classify synthetic dyes extensively to color decorative objects. In fact, Egyptian blue (calcium copper silicate) is considered the world's first synthetic pigment.

Ancient Egypt's many gods and goddesses were common themes on pottery, in textiles, and in their funerary equipment. Gold was easily found throughout ancient Egypt and was more commonly used for decorative art items than silver. Egyptians of this era also perfected the art of gilding, putting a thin layer of gold leaf over

An Egyptian gold statue of the goddess Serket at the Tutankhamun exhibition.

Hieroglyphics were stamped onto various fabrics and papyrus in the Egyptian Renaissance.

wood, metal, or stone, as well as inlaying, the art of inserting small pieces of wood or stone inside larger pieces for decoration.

The Egyptian Renaissance (called "al-Nahda" in Arabic) occurred in the late nineteenth and early twentieth centuries. Politically and intellectually, it was a return to Egypt's heritage and roots after a period of occupation by the Ottoman Turks, the French under Napoleon, and Great Britain. For design, this meant a break from European designs and fabrics and a return to ancient motifs and themes, such as hieroglyphics on fabrics, columns, and gilded art objects.

Today, Egypt is considered a trendsetter in the Arab world, in design as well as in music, cinema, and literature. Some of the best decorative art to come from this region combines a nod to Egypt's illustrious past with modern materials and design techniques.

The Art of the Maasai

The Maasai of eastern Africa are one of the most recognized of the tribes in Africa. These nomadic people, who live in Kenya and Tanzania, are noted for their tall stature, their stoicism, and their fighting prowess. They are also well known for their colorful, woven, and beaded blankets, painted vessels made from gourds, carved wooden masks, and beaded baskets.

WEAPONRY AS DECORATIVE ART

More than 1,300 unique tribes and peoples, not counting subtribes, call Africa home, and they speak more than 3,000 languages. Some might say, even with the vast amount of land in Africa, that conflict among tribes was inevitable. The creation of weapons in Africa far predates the colonial era. From earliest recorded history, African communities were crafting spears, shields, and bows and arrows. Some even forged swords. These were used for ceremonial purposes and prestige, as well as hunting and war.

In Ethiopia, craftsmen made shields from hippo and rhino hide with rounded bumps they worked into the skin when it was still soft and pliable. In East Africa, shields were made of gazelle, buffalo, and lion skins, with the most important warriors obtaining pelts from the most ferocious animals. These items blur the lines between weaponry and art. For example, the Maasai tribe of Kenya made elaborate warrior headdresses of ostrich plumes, called *enkuraru*. Today, many of these former warring implements (and reproductions) hang on the walls of African homes as a reminder of the residents' heritage.

Ethiopian craftsmen made shields from hippo and rhino hide. Shields, like this one, may hang on the walls of African homes.

THE LONG HISTORY OF AFRICAN CARVING AND SCULPTURE

African wood carving and sculpture is a time-honored art that dates back to earliest recorded history. Skilled African carvers created shields, tableware, figures of deities, and ceremonial masks from the trees that grew throughout the sub-Saharan part of the continent. These sculptures range from quite primitive to extremely ornate. Many are adorned with feathers, ivory, bone, and metal.

Of particular note are the carvings of the Mande tribes of West Africa and their broad, flat figures with legs that resemble cylinders, and those of the tribes of Central Africa and their figures with heart-shaped faces and dotted patterns.

Carvings of tribal women.

CONTEMPORARY AFRICAN DECORATIVE ART: MELDING PAST AND PRESENT

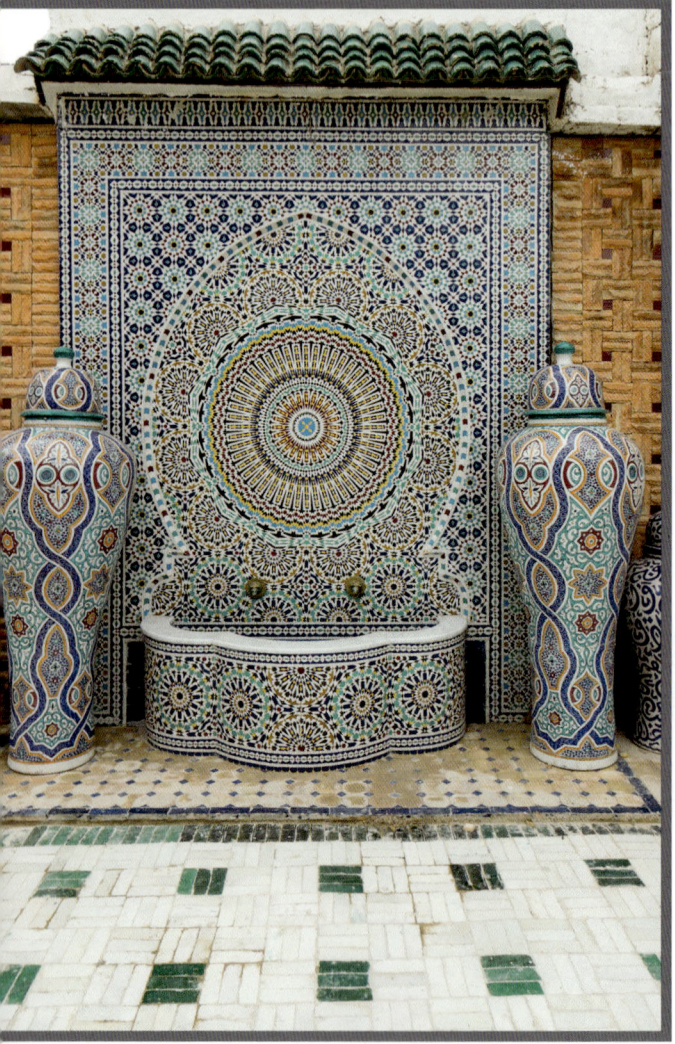

A handmade Moroccan mosaic fountain.

Contemporary African decorative art combines the best elements of traditional, colonial, and modern design. African textiles continue to be popular, and not just to those of African heritage. Runways in Paris and Milan are showing traditional African fabrics, such as *adire* from Yoruba and wax prints from other parts of West Africa, in modern clothing designs. Animal-print patterns, an essential element of African colonial design, are stamped on tabletops or photographed on canvas to hang on walls. Mosaic, a mainstay in Islamic (and North African) design, is moving south of the Sahara Desert and is featured on planters, walls, tabletops, and more. Tight woven patterns, such as those made by the Tutsi of Rwanda, are used in everything from floor coverings to screens and room dividers.

Contemporary African decorative art is also featured in museums around the globe. Prestige auction houses, such as Christie's and Sotheby's, are including more and more African decorative art in their sales as demand for the work of African artists and craftspeople increases.

YORUBA TEXTILES: ANCIENT TECHNIQUES FOR MODERN FASHION

A woman dyes adire cotton.

The Yoruba tribe of Nigeria is noted for its colorful, hand-dyed textiles, especially wall hangings and clothing. The cloth, called *adire* (which means "tie" and "dye" in the Yoruba language), is indigo-dyed cotton cloth with intricate patterns made using resistant-dyeing techniques, such as painting the cloth with cassava paste and stitching raffia cloth onto the fabric before dyeing. *Adire* is still made using most of the same techniques used centuries ago. Examples of Yoruba textile art hang in the Metropolitan Museum of Art in New York City and have been worn by such prominent people as Michelle Obama and actor Lupita Nyong'o.

RAFFIA CLOTH: VERSATILE AND SUSTAINABLE

Raffia is a species of palm tree that grows in central and southern Africa, particularly on the island of Madagascar. The sturdy, durable veins on the underside of this plant's leaves are dried to be used in a variety of household and decorative items, including making hats, baskets, placemats, and textiles. Raffia leaves can grow to be up to 60 feet (18 meters) long. Natural raffia fibers can also be used as decorative garden ties or for wrapping holiday packages. The green building industry has taken note of raffia and has built sustainable support beams and roof coverings from this product.

Raffia can be used to make hats, baskets, placemats, textiles, and clothing, like this dance skirt.

Voodoo figurines at an African market.

THE INFLUENCE OF TRADITIONAL AFRICAN RELIGIONS ON DECORATIVE ART

Africa has had almost as many religious influences as it has had tribes—and there are still more than 1,300 tribes on the continent. North African countries are mostly Islamic and lend their unique slant to traditional calligraphy, glass, and metalwork. Western Africa has Vodun, the native religion that spawned voodoo in Louisiana and parts of the Caribbean. Carved figures and elaborate costumes are closely associated with these beliefs. In other regions, masks, textiles, and drinking vessels and cups play an important role.

European missionaries left less of a mark on Africa's culture and traditions than they did in other parts of the world. Even when Africans converted to Christianity, they clung to many of their traditional ways, including their decorative arts.

AFRICAN MASKS: DECORATIVE, BUT WITH A PURPOSE

African masks are both decorative and useful, and they have influenced Western art and design for more than a century. You can see this in the angular shapes of Cubist paintings and in the modern block designs of mid-twentieth-century architecture. Ceremonial masks are used throughout a wide stretch of Africa, from Guinea and Sierra Leone in the west to Mozambique and Malawi to the east. These masks, which vary from wood to clay to raffia, are used in both religious and life ceremonies, as well as to depict and honor the status of a household (such as one with a top warrior or a town ruler).

A traditional mask from Congo.

CHAPTER 2 ASIA

Some of the world's most important decorative art forms originated in Asia. Chinese, Japanese, Indian, Korean, and Southeast Asian cultures have all contributed greatly to Asian (sometimes called "Eastern" or "Oriental") decorative art. This part of the world is noted for its religious art, particularly images of Hindu and Buddhist deities, and for its many different forms of pottery and intricate wood carvings.

CHINESE DECORATIVE ART: ANCIENT, EVOCATIVE, AND INFLUENTIAL

Chinese decorative art is among the most recognized in the world. The Chinese are arguably the culture with the longest, continuous history of decorative art in the world. Indeed, the word *china* has become synonymous in the West with fine porcelain. The earliest evidence of Chinese art, mostly pottery and sculpture, dates back to 10,000 BCE.

The Chinese pioneered the techniques behind fine porcelain.

In Chinese culture, bamboo represents the spirit of a scholar. It can be used as decorative art in the home, too.

Among the decorative techniques pioneered by the Chinese are lacquerware, fine woven silk, cloisonné enamel, decorative screens painted with extremely detailed landscape murals, carved jade pieces (such as chopstick rests), and, of course, fine porcelain.

Chinese decorative art pieces have often been associated with religion. Early bronze vessels were used for sacrifices to heaven and the gods. Later, as Buddhism became popular in China, metal, ceramic, and stone carvings of the Buddha graced public buildings and homes. Images in Chinese decorative art are largely symbolic. For example, bamboo represents the spirit of a scholar, jade denotes purity and indestructibility, the gnarled pine tree represents survival or old age, and a dragon represents the emperor.

Decorative art, and living in a balanced house environment, is extremely important in the Chinese culture. The concept of yin and yang, or universal complementarity and duality, is also ever-present in Chinese decorative arts. For instance, symmetry is very important in Chinese design, as is placement of objects in a room and the color palette.

Art of all varieties, including the decorative arts, was strongly discouraged during the Mao era in China. However, since the 1980s, art has been reborn in China, with both visual and decorative artists combining traditional techniques with modern materials and themes.

JAPANESE DECORATIVE ART: MINIMALIST AND ELEGANT

Japanese decorative art reflects this culture's ability to adapt. Like many of the other cultures we've discussed, Japan was subject to invasion by a variety of other cultures throughout its history, primarily the Chinese. Gradually, however, the Japanese began to adapt what they'd learned from other cultures and make it their own. For example, after centuries of Buddhism being the primary religion in Japan, Shintoism began to dominate around the ninth century.

Japan has a number of unique decorative art forms. This culture is known for origami, the art of creating beautiful, ethereal objects by folding paper, as well as ceramics, woodblock prints, calligraphy, lacquerware, and sculpture. The Japanese were the original minimalists and Japanese homes, even today, are sparsely furnished, with woven sleeping mats, *shoji* screens, and formal, manicured gardens and koi ponds.

Origami is the art of creating various and beautiful objects by folding paper.

The Japanese tea ceremony is a way to find relief from the noise of daily life.

The Japanese tea ceremony and the lovely ceramic pots and cups that accompany it are a time-honored tradition. Designed to do more than quench the thirst, the tea ceremony was created as a peaceful relief from war and the noise and bustle of daily life. This ceremony has rigid etiquette, with rules that have been passed down through the centuries. It is said that the ceremony is the key to unlocking greater understanding and being open to epiphanies.

Evidence of Japanese pottery dates back to the Neolithic Period (about the eleventh century BCE). Since then, Japanese craftsmen have produced some of the world's best pottery, ceramics, and porcelain. Listed here are just a few of the ceramic styles that have originated in Japan.

- *Banko* **ware**: Stoneware traditionally made in the Yokkaichi region of Japan. Most of these pieces are tea cups, tea pots, and sake vessels.
- *Karatsu* **ware**: Made from clay high in iron, *karatsu* ware is noted for its dark brown hue. It can be glazed or unglazed and is one of three types of pottery most favored for tea ceremonies (with raku ware and *hagi* ware).
- *Raku* **ware**: The type of pottery most often used in tea ceremonies. Raku ware is hand-shaped (rather than thrown), fired at low temperatures, and allowed to cool in the open air.
- *Tobe* **ware**: Thick porcelain, mostly painted in blue-and-white patterns.

DECORATIVE ART FROM THE INDIAN SUBCONTINENT

The Indian subcontinent, which includes the present-day countries of India, Pakistan, Nepal, Bangladesh, Sri Lanka (Ceylon), and Bhutan, has made important and varied contributions to the world's practical arts. India's decorative art history is one of the oldest, dating back to the Harappan civilization (3500–1500 BCE). These early artists and craftspeople made religious and household objects from materials at hand, such as jade, ivory, wood, and stone. This civilization also started India's long history of weaving and textile production.

Over the years, India's textiles have been one of the country's most sought-after exports, from pashmina scarves and shawls from Kashmir to hand-blocked prints from Jaipur to elegant silks and saris from Karnataka in southern India. Silk threads were also used to weave elaborate murals and tapestries, many of which depicted landscapes or Hindu gods and goddesses.

Bidri ware, which originated in the South India city of Bidar, is another decorative art associated with this part of the world. This eight-step process uses a blackened alloy of zinc and copper and inlays it with thin sheets of silver. The

India produces some of the most sought-after exports, like pashmina scarves.

The creation of bidri ware is an intricate, eight-step process that uses a blackened alloy of zinc and copper and inlays it with thin sheets of silver.

results are intricately designed ewers (vase-shaped pitchers), plates, hookahs, pots, and other vessels.

A major port on the Silk Road trading route, the island of Sri Lanka (formerly Ceylon) bears the influences of a variety of cultures. In addition to the British (who ruled the island from the mid-nineteenth to the mid-twentieth century), Sri Lanka was home to Indonesian, Dutch, and Portuguese colonists. In contrast to India, Sri Lanka's people are mostly Buddhist. These factors all mixed together to form a unique collection of decorative art, such as carved wooden masks, terra-cotta and other pottery, and batik fabrics inspired by Indonesian settlers.

Japanese Decorative Art Panels: Form Meets Function

Decorative art panels have been a major part of Japanese interior design for centuries. These panels, many of which are painted with detailed landscapes, calligraphy, and floral paintings, are used as room dividers and to enclose private spaces. They are usually hinged, and some of the more elaborate ones are adorned with gold leaf on the outer edges. Notable artists in this genre include Kanō Sanraku, Sesshūu Tōyō, and Katsushika Hokusai.

BUDDHIST ART: BRINGING RELIGION INTO LIFE

There are more than 500 million Buddhists in the world—about 10 percent of the world's population—the majority of whom live in Asia. Although this religion began in the Indian subcontinent in the fifth century BCE, today there are Buddhists throughout the globe, including large numbers in China, Tibet, Mongolia, Southeast Asia, Sri Lanka, Nepal, and Japan. (India remains largely Hindu.) Buddhist decorative art brings the religion into day-to-day life.

This art genre includes figures of the Buddha, both large and small, as well as lotus flowers and mandalas, graphic symbols that help practitioners focus on the main tenets of Buddhism. Depicting the Buddha as both a man and a god is central to the Buddhist religion. Each culture adapts these symbols a little differently, so a statue of Buddha in Japan will look somewhat different from one in Sri Lanka. Most Buddhist households include a prominent shrine.

Statues of Buddha can be found in Chinese, Tibetan, Mongolian, Southeast Asian, Sri Lankan, and many other Asian homes. Buddha artwork is central to the Buddhist religion.

CAMBODIA: ANGKOR WAT AND MORE

Cambodia, nestled in Southeast Asia among Vietnam, Laos, and Thailand, has a rich cultural history. The Khmer Empire, which ruled the area that is now Cambodia from the early ninth to the fifteenth century, gave the world Angkor Wat and similar impressive and durable edifices. Traditional Cambodian decorative arts include silversmithing, lacquerware, stone carving, ceramics, weaving, mural painting, and kite making (both for decoration and exercise).

Silk weaving in Cambodia uses a complex method of dyeing the weft yarn before the weaving process begins and using this contrasting yarn to create a pattern. Common themes include latticework and stars. Cambodian weavers traditionally use natural dyes to color the fabric, such as black dye from ebony bark, red dye from lac insect nests, and indigo and yellow from prohut bark. These silk fabrics are used for pictorial tapestries (called *pidans*) and for furniture upholstery.

The silk weaving and dyeing process in Cambodia is complex. The weft yarn is dyed before the weaving process begins.

ASIA

HINDU ART: THE BEAUTY OF THE LOTUS

Hinduism began as a world religion around 500 BCE, and today counts more than 1 billion followers, the majority of whom live in India. More than a religion, Hinduism is a way of life, with decorative art woven into the fabric of day-to-day living. Hindu creations include mosaic tiles on floors and walls, flower arrangement, caned seats and backs of chairs, and other furniture, metalwork, and weaving textiles for window coverings, floor mats, and clothing.

In fact, Hinduism names 65 specific arts that are important to followers, including *tandula-kusuma-bali-vikara*, the art of preparing offerings from rice and flowers; *suci-vaya-karma*, the art of needlework and weaving; and *takshana*, the art of carpentry. The lotus flower, a common symbol in Hindu homes, denotes purity, beauty, and prosperity. Hindu gods and goddesses are often depicted on Hindu decorative art. Many of these figures have extra limbs, which implies they are good at doing a lot of tasks at the same time.

The lotus flower is a sign of purity, beauty, and prosperity in Hinduism.

IN NEPAL ART BORN OF ISOLATION

The Himalayan mountain nation of Nepal was largely cut off from the rest of the world until modern times. As a result, it developed its own unique art forms. Located between China and India, Nepal is home to eight of the world's ten tallest mountains, including Mount Everest. Decorative art here favors useful and religious— rather than strictly ornamental—objects. However, Nepalese artists are adept at using color and natural dyes to create attractive as well as functional items like blankets, pottery, carved wooden and bronze figures, and woven wall hangings and mandalas. The diverse cultural mixture of peoples in Nepal also contributes to making Nepalese designs unique and appealing.

A Nepalese man works on a traditional Mani slate stone.

LACQUERWARE: FROM SAP TO ELEGANT BEAUTY

Lacquerware is commonly recognized as trays and bowls, boxes, or urns, but it isn't uncommon to see lacquer-coated furniture, too.

Lacquer-coated furniture and carved decorative pieces have a long history in both China and Japan, dating back to earliest recorded history. Although the materials may vary, the common denominator in lacquerware is the clear, shiny, durable coating, made with urushiol-based substance known as "lacquer" that is derived from the sap of the Chinese lacquer tree. Some lacquerware is inlaid with mother-of-pearl or dusted with gold or silver leaf before the coating is applied. Common lacquerware items include serving trays and bowls, tables, decorative boxes, and urns. In Japan, lacquerware is referred to as *shikki*; in Myanmar (formerly Burma), it is *yun-de*; and in Vietnam, it is *son mai*.

JADE: JEWELS FROM THE EARTH

Jade is an English term that describes the minerals nephrite and jadeite. It is most commonly seen in shades of green but is also found in white, lavender, and even a light pinkish hue. Jade is noted for being smooth

Jade is a very hard mineral so it takes a lot of work to make it smooth. That is what makes jade artwork so beautiful and special.

and opalesque, almost opaque. Jade has been used in Chinese decorative art since the beginning of recorded history, although its early use was generally restricted to tribal leaders and rulers. Jade is extremely hard and cannot be worked and cut with traditional tools. It must be rubbed vigorously into the desired shape. That makes the intricate flowers, implements, and jewelry made from this material even more valuable and astonishing.

CHINESE POTTERY, FROM DYNASTY TO DYNASTY

The Chinese have been noted throughout history for their excellent pottery, ceramics, and porcelain. In fact, in the West, such objects are called "china." Chinese pottery dates back to more than two centuries before the Christian era. The Chinese were the first to use a kiln to fire clay pottery, and they pioneered the use of natural dyes that would

Chinese pottery is created by forming clay into its desired shape and then placing it in a kiln to fire it at a high temperature.

stand up to that intense heat. Chinese pottery includes dinnerware, urns, large pots for flowers and trees, and vases. It is generally categorized by the dynasty during which it was created, such as Tang, Yuan, Ming, or Qin.

CHAPTER 3 EUROPE

Europe has contributed greatly to the history of decorative arts. From the gilded edges of the Renaissance era to the sleek lines of the Art Deco Period, furniture and decorative objects from France, Italy, Holland, and Germany have set the pace for home décor around the globe. This part of the world has introduced us to design masters from Leonardo da Vinci to Hector Guimard, from Carlo Bugatti to René Lalique.

RENAISSANCE EUROPE: A REBIRTH OF ART AND DESIGN

The Renaissance was a lengthy period of renewed interest in art, design, and architecture in Europe. It followed the austerity of the Middle Ages and spanned from the early fourteenth century to the seventeenth century. The first stirrings of the Renaissance era began in Italy with such masters of multiple arts and sciences as Leonardo da Vinci and Michelangelo. In fact, it was this type of artist and thinker that gave birth to the term "Renaissance man."

Renaissance design and architecture made use of classical elements from Greek and Roman design, as well as art and design elements from biblical stories. The wealthy families of Europe, such as the French kings and the Medici family of Florence, embraced and supported Renaissance artists, as did the Roman Catholic Church, which commissioned numerous paintings and sculptures to adorn its churches and cathedrals. Michelangelo's mural on the ceiling of the Vatican's Sistine Chapel dates from this time period. Arches, columns, and domes are common architectural elements of the Renaissance era. Two good examples of this style are St. Peter's Basilica in Vatican City and the Florence Cathedral.

Michelangelo's mural on the ceiling of the Sistine Chapel is one of the most famous in Italian history. This painting reflects the style of the Renaissance era.

Much of the Renaissance architecture includes arches, columns, and domes, as seen here at the Florence Cathedral.

The Renaissance movement arrived in France around the fifteenth century and is responsible for the Louvre Museum (formerly a palace), as well as the many classic chateaux along the Loire River (that era's answer to the country house). French Renaissance designers added highly manicured gardens as an extension of the interior design, and estate owners would compete for the most elaborate garden design.

Holland became interested in the Renaissance by the mid-fifteenth century, influenced in part by Dutch trade with Venice. The Dutch modified the decorative designs of France and Italy by adding very dark, almost black, carved furnishings and colorful decorative tile work.

Renaissance Art in the Vatican

Some of the best examples of Renaissance art can be found in Vatican City in Rome. In addition to Michelangelo's mural on the ceiling of the Sistine Chapel, you can find Michelangelo's *The Last Judgment* behind the Sistine Chapel altar; Caravaggio's *The Entombment of Christ* in the Vatican museums; and Raphael's *The School of Athens*, also in the Vatican museums. In addition to these masterpieces, there are Renaissance architectural landmarks, such as Bernini's design of St. Peter's Square.

EIGHTEENTH-CENTURY EUROPEAN DESIGN: FROM BAROQUE EXCESS TO NEOCLASSICAL RESTRAINT

Eighteenth-century Europe saw a diverse progression of design styles. The Baroque style began in the late seventeenth century and lasted well into the eighteenth century. This highly ornate style was the successor to the Renaissance and maintained that era's emphasis on church art and grandeur. Baroque style is best known for its exuberant detail, deep color, and use of contrast—all of which worked together to create a sense of awe.

The interior of this living room showcases the vintage designs of Baroque and Rococo styles.

This castle in the Czech Republic displays the classical Biedermeier furnishings and décor from the beginning of the nineteenth century.

Rococo style, also known as Late Baroque, emerged in France and Italy during the 1730s and quickly spread to Germany, Russia, and central Europe. Rococo is known for elaborate, embellished designs; gilding; curved lines; and trompe l'oeil (optical illusion) murals and designs. Rococo was slower coming to Britain, where it was known as "French style." Among the notable British contributions to Rococo are the chairs and other furnishings of Thomas Chippendale. Rococo style ended around 1750 as French philosophers of the day began to decry the excesses of the nobility.

Rococo was followed by a resurgence of Neoclassicism, a revival of the timeless elements of Greek and Roman design, such as columns, stone façades, angular borders, and bas-relief. Neoclassicism manifested itself as Empire and Louis XVI styles in France, as Biedermeier furnishings in Austria, and as Regency style in Britain.

Chinoiserie was a brief, but very popular, style in France and Britain during the mid-eighteenth century. Inspired by the designs of the Far East and China (at least what Europeans imagined they were), chinoiserie featured lacquered furniture, large ceramic and porcelain urns and vases, colorful Asian print silk fabrics, and dragon motifs.

NINETEENTH-CENTURY EUROPEAN DESIGN: ANCIENT MOTIFS GIVE WAY TO MODERN ARTISANSHIP

If the design styles of France dominated eighteenth-century design, Great Britain dominated the nineteenth century. As the British Empire reached its zenith, colonists brought back materials and design motifs from the four corners of the globe. In this way, Chinese and Islamic art worked their way into a variety of nineteenth-century design styles.

Early nineteenth-century European design is associated with Greek Revival, and elements from Greek and Roman mythology made their way onto decorative objects and home décor. That movement gave way to Gothic Revival, with a resurgence of vaulted arches, religious art, and statuary. London's Houses of Parliament buildings are good examples of the architecture of this period.

London's House of Parliament is a perfect example of architecture from the Gothic Revival.

The Arts and Crafts movement featured many designs that were made by homeowners. Pictured here is a wallpaper design made by famous textile designer William Morris featuring a trellis.

Of course, by the middle of the nineteenth century, Victorian design took over British decorative art and architecture (see page 40). At the same time, Art Nouveau (French for "new art") was the primary design style in France. This style is noted for its curving lines, fanciful motifs, and bold blocks of color. Some of the best remaining examples of Art Nouveau architecture include the classic Metro stations in Paris, designed by Hector Guimard.

The Arts and Crafts movement began at the end of the nineteenth century and provided a stark contrast to the ornate and somewhat fussy Victorian designs. The Arts and Crafts movement featured straight lines, built-in furniture, leaded glass lamps, and a variety of traditional handicrafts. This design style, which grew out of the design work of William Morris and John Ruskin, stressed function as well as beauty. Morris admonished clients to "have nothing in your house that you do not know to be useful or believe to be beautiful."

VICTORIAN DECORATIVE ARTS

The Victorian era began with the 18-year-old Victoria's advent as Queen of England in 1837 and ended roughly with her death in 1901. Because this was a prosperous time in Britain, which was at the height of the Empire era, Victorian decorative arts are notably showy, expensive, and heavily adorned.

Victorian-style homes are noted for their decorative moldings; turrets, porches, widow's walks, and other architectural embellishments; and the inclusion of the most important room of the era—the parlor. Interior spaces in the Victorian era were heavily furnished and accessorized, with artwork and other decorative pieces covering the majority of the wall space. Rooms were generally painted somber, dark colors. This era also corresponded with new mass-production techniques for wallpaper and printed wall coverings.

Victorian interiors, like this one, tended to be heavily furnished and decorated with dark colors.

ART DECO: SO MODERN, SO FRENCH

One of the best known design movements to have emerged from Europe, Art Deco was officially named in Paris in 1925, as a shortened version of the French *arts décoratifs*. Whereas Modernism emphasized function over decoration, Art Deco sought to make items beautiful and glamorous as well as functional. Popular in the 1920s and 1930s, Art Deco design was a combination of several different styles and included furniture, household objects, transportation, and even buildings. Well-known examples of Art Deco architecture include New York City's Chrysler Building, and the Champs-Elysees Theatre and Palais de Chaillot in Paris.

Art Deco is noted for its sleek, rounded lines; its use of shiny metals and the then-new Bakelite plastic, among other materials; and the fine artisianship of its items. Noted Art Deco artists, designers, and architects include Henri Sauvage, René Lalique, and Paul Landowski (the sculptor of *Christ the Redeemer* in Rio de Janeiro). Though it originated in France, the Art Deco movement quickly spread around the globe, and examples can be found from Mexico to China to South America. The Art Deco era ended with the advent of World War II, when materials became scarce and people lacked money for fancy furniture.

Art Deco spread from France around the world. The interior of the Palacio de Bellas Artes in Mexico City, shown here, is an excellent example of the design movement.

EUROPE

SIMPLY DANISH, WITH GERMAN INSPIRATION

Danish Modern design emerged as a direct result of the German Bauhaus movement, which advocated the seamless integration of decorative and industrial design as well as a community of skilled workers from all classes laboring side by side on a design project.

Danish Modern, conceived by Kaare Klint in the period between the two world wars, embraced Minimalist lines that fit the contours of the human body. Klint, the head of the furniture department at the Architecture School of the Royal Danish Academy of Fine Arts, encouraged his students to emphasize form and function instead of ornamentation and embellishment. His teachings formed the basis for the Danish Modern movement. Although teakwood is perhaps the material most associated with Danish Modern, other materials such as hard plastic (often white), other types of wood, and steel were also frequently used. Danish Modern design was not limited to furniture; Danish Modern lamps, dishes, and cutlery were also produced.

American companies obtained licenses to produce classic Danish Modern designs shortly after World War II, leading to this design style's popularity in the United States in the 1950s and 1960s. This type of furniture was also affordable and represented a break from the heavier, dark wood pieces favored by the previous generation.

The Danish Museum of Art & Design features an assortment of chairs made with Danish Modern design in mind.

CASSONI: MARRIAGE HOPE CHESTS

Cassoni are large marriage chests made popular in Italy during the late Middle Ages. By the fifteenth century, these decorated "hope" chests were the most important pieces of furniture that a family could own. Wealthy merchants competed with each other to see who could have the most beautiful *cassone* constructed. The family amassed household goods to put in the *cassone* during a daughter's childhood, and the chest was given to the bride on her wedding day to take into her marriage. It was customarily placed in the bridal suite on the night of the wedding. *Cassoni* were often adorned with family crests and other symbols that reflected a family's position and power, such as animals, arms, banners, and crowns.

Marriage chests, also referred to as cassoni, held household goods during a woman's childhood that would later be given to her on her wedding day to take into her new marriage.

THE ART OF THE FAMILY CREST

The art of the family crest has been around practically since the beginning of recorded history. However, this art form rose to new heights in Europe during the High Middle Ages (from 1000 to around 1250 CE). These family crests, or coats of arms, almost always included a shield, a helmet, and a crest, and they were sometimes adorned with badges, supporters (the griffins or other creatures on the sides of the crest), banners, and mottoes. They were a not-so-subtle way of displaying family pride and strength and were usually prominently displayed in homes and on armor. In fact, one of the original uses of the family crest was to aid in identifying the person inside a suit of heavy body armor. Although such armor is now found only in museums, the idea of family crests has survived to this day.

A variety of family coats of arms found in a church.

Europe

THREE SCOTTISH BROTHERS NAMED ADAM

Named for three Scottish brothers (James Adam, Robert Adam, and John Adam), Adam style, also called Adamesque, is a form of Neoclassical interior design and architecture that was popular among the upper classes in Europe during the mid- to late nineteenth century. Adam style is noted for its integration of architecture, furnishings, and fittings—all designed by a single architect/designer. The Adam style features a dramatic color palette, with vibrant greens, reds, and gold, and the use of curved doorways, ceilings, and plasterwork. This design style was replaced in Britain by the Regency style in 1795, and in France and Russia by the French Empire style around the same time. Examples of the Adam style can still be found in Great Britain, including Syon House in London and Derby House in London's Grosvenor Square.

These plans show the interior design elements used inside the Derby House in London's Grosvenor Square.

A CRAZE FOR EGYPTIAN STYLE

Lenin's Mausoleum in Moscow is a top tourist attraction as well as an architectural example of the Egyptian Revival.

Egyptian Revival became popular in France, Britain, and the rest of western Europe following Napoleon's conquest of Egypt and his subsequent defeat by Britain's Admiral Nelson at the Battle of the Nile in 1798. The large concentration of Europeans in Egypt during that time sparked a huge interest in Egyptian art, artifacts, and architecture. Egyptian Revival design remained popular through the mid-nineteenth century and is noted for its use of papyrus columns, grand stone facades, and depictions of pharaoh heads and other Egyptian symbols as adornments. Examples from this era include the Obelisk of Luxor that sits in the middle of the Place de la Concorde in Paris; the Egyptian House in Penzance, England; Lenin's Mausoleum in Moscow, which borrows design elements from the Pyramid of Djoser; and the Pyramid Theatre in Manchester, England.

CHAPTER 4 LATIN AMERICA AND THE CARIBBEAN

Decorative art in Latin America and the Caribbean region draws from pre-Columbian, colonial, and modern influences. Some of the world's most prized silverwork and textiles come from this part of the globe. In addition, the mélange of cultures that have touched this region, from Mayan to French and Spanish to Rastafarian, have all left their unique impressions.

PRE-COLUMBIAN DECORATIVE ART

"Pre-Columbian art" refers to visual and decorative art that predates Christopher Columbus's arrival in the New World, roughly defined as the Caribbean islands and North, Central, and South America. It lasted between the late fifteenth and early sixteenth centuries. (Pre-Columbian in this context refers to Christopher Columbus, not the modern country of Colombia.) Before the arrival of the Spanish and other western European explorers, this region was peopled with a number of advanced civilizations, including the Maya, the Inca, and the Arawak, Taino, and Caribe tribes. Each developed its own unique decorative art forms, frequently using the vast natural treasures of gold, silver, and gemstones found in this part of the world.

The Maya, who lived in Mexico and Central America, were known for their carvings, textiles, and masks embellished with gemstones such as lapis lazuli

This mask is handmade and adorned with natural stones and minerals.

The Inca were expert potters who made vases and statuettes.

and malachite. More than mere decoration, these items served to tie present generations of Mayans to their ancestors via stories depicted in the carvings and weaving. Mayan carving and textiles continue to be prized today. (See the section on Guatemalan textiles.)

The Inca, who lived high in the Andes Mountains from what is now Peru to the tip of present-day Chile and Argentina, were expert potters and silver- and goldsmiths. From cities like Machu Picchu and Cusco, they created bowls, urns, and other thrown pottery with geometric designs and images of animals and plants. Few silver and gold items from this period still exist, because most were melted down by the conquering Spanish. However, the few pieces that have found their way to museums show that the Inca were skilled at stamping and etching intricate designs onto metal boxes, plates, and other decorative items.

The Taino tribe and the Carib people, also known as the Kalinago tribe, were the indigenous people of the Lesser Antilles, a group of islands in the Caribbean. These societies left a rich legacy of woodworking and were particularly known for carving small statues (often made to honor their many gods), elaborate footstools, and dugout canoes.

SPANISH COLONIAL DECORATIVE ART

When the Europeans arrived in the New World, their greed, land-grabbing, and diseases like smallpox that they brought with them all but erased the indigenous peoples from what is now Central America, South America, and the Caribbean. Most of these invaders were Spanish, and with their aggressive ways they also brought the decorative art forms of southern Europe, which they quickly adapted to the materials that could be easily found in the New World.

These Spanish colonial art forms included carved, solid furniture made from pine; colorful tile work and mosaics that the Spanish had earlier adapted from Islamic art; iron and metalwork, including cast-iron cabinet hardware and heavy, ornate chandeliers; and interior courtyards and gardens, adorned with colorful

Colorful tile work and mosaics, adapted from Islamic art, was a popular art form and type of décor in the Spanish colonial era.

Statues of the Virgin Mary were, and are, a common theme in Catholic homes in Latin America.

flowers and plants that grew abundantly in the Americas. Spanish colonial homes had massive stucco fireplaces, often decorated with ceramic tile, as well as large exposed wooden support beams, usually finished in a dark stain. Frequently, colonists would bring small decorative items from home, such as candlesticks and small tapestries, and these items became a permanent part of what we call Spanish colonial design.

The introduction of Catholicism also influenced decorative art in this region, with more than 15,000 churches built in Latin America between 1650 and 1800. Most homes had at least one cross on the wall, as well as small religious shrines and statues of Jesus, Mary, and a patron saint. This religious zeal also helped to create a somber, more conservative mood in the colonies, and the darker, less vibrant designs of Spanish colonial homes reflect this solemnness.

CREATING A MODERN LATIN AMERICAN STYLE

Decorative artists in modern Latin America have taken elements from the region's indigenous and colonial pasts and incorporated those of present-day Europe and the United States to create a unique and distinctly Latin style. In fact, art scholars have coined the term *Modernismo* to describe this art movement, which began in the early twentieth century.

Folk art, such as hand-thrown pottery and metalwork, continues to be an important part of the decorative art landscape in Peru and Chile, although the designs are now more contemporary. Often, black-and-white motifs replace traditional colorful themes. Particularly sought after is Chulucanas pottery from the region of Peru bearing the same name. Silverwork, such as filigreed serving platters, candlesticks, and flatware, continues to be an important part of this region's design heritage, although the lines on these items today are somewhat simpler and sleeker than they have been in the past.

In the Caribbean, the independence movements of the 1950s and 1960s inspired the island people to rediscover their indigenous and African ancestry and the art of their ancestors. In Jamaica, this movement has been labeled "Intuitive

Chulucanas pottery is more contemporary and is made in black and white.

The colorful, festive clothing in the Caribbean is a way of defining rank and status but also a way of boosting one's mood.

art." Intuitive art often includes religious elements from the Jamaican Rastafarian sects that trace their roots back to ancient Egypt and Ethiopia. Frequently, Intuitive artists create sculpture and decorative art objects from discarded objects like oil drums and old tin roofs.

Fiber art has also made a resurgence in the Caribbean. In many Caribbean cultures, apparel defines a person's rank and status. Thus colorful, festive clothing is a way of boosting not only one's mood but his or her standing in the community. Knitted hats and shawls—as well as fiber art used as wall hangings—are becoming increasingly popular, not only on the islands but as exports.

The Influence of the Indigenous Carib and Arawak Tribes

The Arawak and Carib tribes were the original inhabitants of what are now the Bahamas and Caribbean Islands, as well as parts of Central and South America. The two tribes couldn't have been more different, however. The Arawak were a warring tribe, whereas the Carib people were peaceful. Surviving Carib and Arawak design elements include colorful woven textiles and intricately carved wooden tools and housewares. Both tribes were wiped out battling European settlers— and by the diseases brought to the islands by these invaders. However, their influence can still be seen in items like Guatemalan textiles and Jamaican wood carvings.

THE INCA: A GLORIOUS ANCIENT CIVILIZATION

The Inca Empire was the largest in pre-Columbian America, extending from the southern part of what is now Chile to modern-day Peru to the north. The historic cities of Machu Picchu and Cusco, Peru, were built by the Inca. This civilization lasted from the early thirteenth century until its last city was conquered by Spanish explorers in 1572. Incan decorative art is very elaborate and focuses on pottery, textiles, and metalwork.

Pottery was painted in geometric patterns using natural dyes of several hues. Popular motifs included animals (particularly cats), birds, and waves. Metalwork was made mostly from silver and gold found in the Andes Mountains. Cooking vessels, candelabras, vases, and statuary were often made of solid, 24-karat gold. The Spanish legend of "El Dorado," a city made of gold, likely comes from the looting of Cusco and the vast number of golden objects the explorers found there.

In addition to gold cooking vessels, candelabras, vases, and statuary, the Inca people also made religious objects for their homes.

SOUTH AMERICAN SILVER: DETAILED AND ELEGANT DESIGNS

The Inca weren't the only ones to create silver decorative objects. The rich mines of the Andes Mountains and surrounding areas made it a go-to material for crafting everything from jewelry to weapons to decorations for the home. From the time of the Inca to the present, the Andes region is known for its delicately etched silver boxes of all sizes, hand-stamped silver bowls and platters, and sculpture.

Themes reflect nature—such as animals, flowers, the sun and the moon, traditional gods, and fish and birds—and the heritage of the people who still inhabit the Andes Mountains. Most silverwork from this region is very detailed, with interlacing vines and rays that lead the eye from one vignette to the next.

A South American bowl stamped with a geometric design.

GUATEMALAN TEXTILES AND CARVINGS: SURVIVING THE CONQUEST

The beautiful, brightly colored woven textiles produced in the Central American country of Guatemala come from the country's Mayan heritage. Located southeast of Mexico and spanning the entire isthmus between the Caribbean Sea and the Pacific Ocean, Guatemala was home to the Maya from around 250 CE until the society was all but wiped out by Spanish explorers and disease in the late seventeenth century.

Descendants of the Maya still populate Central America and have kept their art forms, including weaving, alive. Guatemalan textiles are mostly cotton and are noted for their loose weave, their explosive colors, and their geometric patterns.

Wood carving is another time-honored art form in Guatemala. Most common are bright, whimsical, hand-carved animals, bowls, masks, and candleholders, made of cedar and other indigenous woods. Because Guatemala is predominantly Roman Catholic, carvings with religious themes and figures of saints are also often used as decorations.

Guatemalan textiles keep with tradition and are made on a loom.

RELIGIOUS DECORATIVE ART IN LATIN AMERICA

Wood carving in Latin America is just as prevalent as it was in the past. In Peru, these carved-wood statues represent the arrival of the first Inca civilization.

The Spanish conquest of Central and South America left a definitive mark. Because conflict and European diseases all but erased the indigenous peoples of these regions, the majority of the inhabitants of this area after the sixteenth century were influenced by Spanish, and later Portuguese, culture. That means the majority of them were Roman Catholics. Even the indigenous people who survived the arrival of the Europeans were taught by friars and often converted to Catholicism. Thus, native decorative skills, such as wood carving and silversmithing, were used to create religious icons for homes and furniture, such as crosses, screens, pews, pulpits, and altars, for the increasing number of churches in the region.

HAITIAN PAINTING AND DECORATIVE ARTS: BORN OF FREEDOM

A Haitian artist paints using simple folk design and vibrant color.

Haiti, located on the western part of the Caribbean island of Hispaniola, was the first island in the region to abolish slavery, end colonialism, and become an independent nation (in 1803). This head start on independence gave a freer rein to creative expression here than in other parts of the Caribbean that were still heavily influenced by colonialism. Nowhere is this freedom more apparent than in Haitian painting. This art form is noted throughout the art world for its simple folk designs and use of vibrant color. Haitian paintings usually depict everyday scenes, such as women at the market, families sharing a meal, or a mother tending her children.

LATIN AMERICA AND THE CARIBBEAN

JAMAICAN DECORATIVE ART REFLECTS THE ISLAND'S HISTORY

These Jamaican wood carvings are meant to be displayed on one's wall.

Jamaican decorative art reflects the island's many cultural influences. One of the largest islands in the Caribbean, Jamaica was inhabited by the Arawak and Carib tribes before Christopher Columbus landed here during one of his voyages and brought an influx of Spanish colonists. Later, the British conquered the Spanish on Jamaica and ruled the island for more than 300 years, until the island was granted independence in 1962.

Jamaican decorative art favors carved wooden figures, furniture, and wall hangings, as well as creative metalwork. The island is also well known for furniture manufacturing. Elegant "Georgian" furniture designs from teak, mahogany, and other hardwoods were shipped throughout the globe during the late eighteenth and early nineteenth centuries.

THE VIBRANT TEXTILES OF THE ANDES

The Andes region of South America is known for more than its silverwork. This region, which extends from Venezuela in the north to the tip of Chile and Argentine in the south, has produced textiles in vibrant colors since the pre-Columbian Period. Andean textiles, which are made from cotton and/or llama and alpaca wool, are used for everything from ceremonial clothing to wall hangings and floor coverings. They are made in much the same way today as they were more than 1,000 years ago. The people of this region pioneered several weaving techniques, including triple weave.

A woman sells a variety of Andean textiles.

CHAPTER 5 MIDDLE EAST

The area from the Mediterranean to the Ural Mountains, from southern Egypt to the tip of the Sinai Peninsula, and from the Bosporus to the Caspian Sea is collectively known as the Middle East. This region has been home to a variety of empires over the centuries, from the Romans to the Byzantines to the Ottomans. All left their mark, as has this region's mostly Islamic population. Hand-knotted area rugs from this part of the globe are arguably the best in the world, and Islamic glass combines techniques from several cultures to make a beautiful and unique product.

THE ART OF ISLAM

The arrival of Islam in the seventh century CE transformed decorative art in the Middle East. Although not exclusively religious, Islamic laws frown on adornments that are not for the glory of Allah. Therefore, even if Islamic art objects are not designed specifically for use in a mosque or religious shrine, they almost always have a religious component.

One of the most singular, and most beautiful, of the Islamic decorative arts is calligraphy. Grown out of the art of writing and illustrating the Qu'ran, Islamic calligraphy has evolved into a beautiful art expression, often with a saying written so that the script forms an image. In addition to wall hangings and scrolls, Islamic calligraphy can be found on coins, ceramic tiles, metalwork, and framed miniatures. Because the world of Islamic is diverse, Islamic calligraphy can be found in a variety of languages as well, including Arabic, Turkish, Persian, and Urdu (the official language of Pakistan).

A man creates Islamic calligraphy for the Qu'ran.

A Muslim woman creates a carpet. Rugs and carpets from this region are used in homes for prayer.

Rugs and carpets from this region, used in homes as well as for prayer, are world-renowned. Many, especially those from Iran, have Islamic designs and themes. In contrast to Western religious art, Islamic art and design generally focuses on floral and geometric forms, rather than on figures (having figures in a design is feared to be idolatry).

Islamic metalwork is unique in that it usually emphasizes one object, such as a tree or a flower, rather than a person. Bronze and brass hammered pieces are traditionally inlaid with tiny silver or gold pieces to create a pattern. Popular objects include swords, ewers, and candlesticks.

BYZANTINE DESIGN: INSPIRED BY THE ORTHODOX CHURCH

The Byzantine Empire was the continuation of the Roman Empire of antiquity and survived the fall of Rome by more than 1,000 years. At its zenith, the Byzantine Empire included parts of North Africa, Egypt, Greece, the Middle East, and Turkey. Based in Byzantium (later called Constantinople and Istanbul), this culture developed its own design style, influenced in large part by the Eastern Orthodox Church.

Highlights of Byzantine design include intricate mosaic designs, many with a religious theme; the use of bold colors; and carved ivory figures, triptychs, and bas-relief panels. Many Byzantine objects are gilded, and these works also carried forward the classic design elements of ancient Rome, such as columns and geometric designs.

The Byzantine design included intricate mosaic designs. Many of these mosaics included a religious theme.

The throne of Archbishop Maximianus was made during the Byzantine Empire.

Square, intricately carved chairs, many adorned with gems, along with silk and velvet drapes and tapestries, were a common furnishing in the homes of wealthy Byzantine citizens. This was also the age of relics, and elaborate gold and silver reliquaries were made to contain these objects.

In home design, vaulted ceilings and arched doorways were the norm, and frescoes—elaborate scenes painted directly on walls—were frequently used. Byzantine design continued to be used throughout other parts of the Christian East, most notably in Russia, long after the fall of the Byzantine Empire in the mid-fifteenth century. St. Basil's Cathedral in Moscow is an excellent example of later Byzantine design and architecture.

A DECORATIVE ARTS RENAISSANCE IN THE MIDDLE EAST

The conservative Islamic regimes in the Middle East have changed the look of Middle Eastern decorative art, but they haven't erased it. Many parts of this multifaceted region are having an art renaissance, both in the visual and decorative arts. In Turkey, after decades of European-style design, young designers are incorporating traditional Turkish (and Ottoman) motifs, such as kilim patterns and symmetrical florals, in pottery, rugs, and interior design.

Israeli decorative art provides yet another dimension to Middle Eastern design. Here, modern art and traditional Judaica have come together to create a new and exciting art form. In addition, colorful, woven textiles from Israel are

Kilim motifs are incorporated into pottery, rugs, and interior design.

Israeli decorative art brings modern art and traditional Judaica together.

appearing both on world fashion runways and as bedspreads, tapestries, and floor coverings.

Elsewhere in the Middle East, Dubai, Qatar, and other Gulf nations are experiencing a building boom, with modern architecture and interior design that evokes the sea that is ever-present on the landscape.

Calligraphy: Writing as Decorative Art

Calligraphy, or elaborate and decorative cursive writing, is often used as art in the Middle East. In fact, some sources call it the most important and most influential form of Islamic art. Though calligraphy as art is undeniably beautiful, even to those who do not read Arabic, the principle aim of such art is to transmit a message. Most such messages are passages from the Qu'ran.

THE OTTOMAN EMPIRE AND ITS DECORATIVE LEGACY

The Ottoman Empire ruled much of the Middle East and beyond from the fourteenth century until the early twentieth century. At its most powerful, the Ottoman Empire included parts of North Africa, Egypt, and Persia, as well as present-day Greece, Austria, Turkey, Ukraine, Russia, and Saudi Arabia. Based in Constantinople/Istanbul, the Ottoman Empire combined influences from all reaches of its realm to create a decorative art style all its own. Design from this time period draws heavily on Byzantine style as well as ancient Persian and Egyptian art. The Ottoman sultans, particularly Suleiman the Magnificent (1494–1622), were great patrons of the arts and even built workshops adjacent to their palaces for struggling artisans.

Decorative art from the Ottoman Empire is noted for hand-knotted, woven carpets; colorful tile work; ornate furniture with elaborate inlays; calligraphy as art; and *ebru*, the traditional art of paper marbling. One of the great contributions of the Ottoman era was taking traditional Islamic art and introducing materials found in the outlying areas of the empire.

The Ottoman Empire often displayed the decorative art called ebru. The traditional art of paper marbling is still used today.

A shop sells antique carpets and kilims.

RUGS: A MAINSTAY OF THE MIDDLE EAST

Perhaps the most widely recognized contributions in decorative art from the Middle East are the beautiful rugs that come from this region. Hand-knotted, naturally dyed area rugs have been a mainstay of this region's décor for centuries and can be made of wool, silk, or cotton. However, rugs from diverse areas of the Middle East are distinctly different from one another.

Persian rugs (from today's Iran and Afghanistan) are noted for their elaborate designs, many of which have a center medallion. They are often named for the towns in which they are made, such as Tabriz, Kerman, and Kashan. Rugs from Turkey, also called Anatolian rugs (after the region where they are made), are noted for their geometric designs. Kilim rugs, produced throughout the countries of the former Ottoman Empire, are flat-woven, generally decorative rugs or prayer rugs (as opposed to floor rugs), although they have been adopted as floor coverings in Western households.

PERSIAN POTTERY: STILL MADE THE OLD-FASHIONED WAY

Pottery making in the area that is now Iran dates back to the seventh century BCE. Early pieces were made using clay mixed with engobe, a white slippery substance that can be used to create a natural pattern and to help dyes run true to color. Today, pottery, especially around the city of Kalpuregan, is still made using the old methods, which are passed down through the generations from mother to daughter. Unlike pottery from other parts of the world, Persian pottery is formed by hand, not thrown using a potter's wheel.

The advent of Islam and its prohibition of luxury metal objects on the table created a new, extensive market for pottery made in the Middle East. Persian artists developed the art of lusterware, a process that adds an iridescent shine to pottery. Much of this Islamic pottery was inscribed with verses from the Qu'ran or other inspirational sayings.

The style of pottery making made in the city of Kalpuregan has been passed down since the seventh century BCE.

CERAMIC TILES HAVE A LONG HISTORY IN THE MIDDLE EAST

Ceramic and glass tiles from the Middle East, frequently referred to as mosaic, are small pieces assembled with mortar to create a design, a portrait, or a mural. Most mosaic tiles are flat; some are smooth, and some are rough or tex-

Jerusalem's Dome of the Rock can be seen from afar. Its golden ceramic mosaic dome sits atop the building.

tured. Mosaic has been used in decorative art in the Middle East since about the third century BCE and peaked around the eighth century CE. This art form was later adopted by western European and North African artisans. Examples of mosaic art include the Dome of the Rock in Jerusalem and the Tomb of Hafez in Shiraz, Iran.

An arabesque stone relief.

ARABESQUE: A POPULAR DESIGN MOTIF, FEATURING VINES

The word arabesque, French for "Arabic style," refers to a form of design often used in the Middle East, though it is not exclusive to the area. An object with arabesques has many carved, drawn, or etched interwoven tendrils—vines or lines that work together to form a design themselves. Arabesque can be found in the Islamic world as early as the eighth century, when this type of design moved from decoration on scrolls to ceramic tile design. This type of design can be found on rugs, pottery, tiles, ceilings, and paintings.

ISLAMIC GLASS: MADE WITH A VARIETY OF TECHNIQUES

Although not as well known throughout the world as Western art glass, Islamic glass artists have made a strong contribution to the art glass world. Begun around the eighth century, Islamic glass focused primarily on glass vessels to be used in religious contexts, such as hanging oil lamps, cups, and ewers. Islamic glass is noted for its translucent quality and for thread trailing, a technique where an artist used threads of molten glass to create a motif on the face of a glass piece. Another popular Islamic glass technique was using enameled glass, where powdered enamel is used to decorate a glass vessel.

This glass lamp was made in the Middle East in approximately 1360 CE.

THE DECORATIVE ART OF ISRAEL

Brass candlesticks are common objects of Judaica.

Israeli decorative art stands apart from that of its many Arabic neighbors. Although this country's art uses many of the same materials, much of Israeli decorative art falls into the category of Judaica, comprising beautiful, hand-crafted objects that are used in Jewish rituals, such as observing the Sabbath or at the Feast of Passover. Objects of Judaica include pitchers, candlesticks, calligraphy art, menorahs, kiddush cups, and spice boxes.
Common materials were silver, nickel, pewter, china, and porcelain.

Before Israel became an independent state in 1948, the region was known as Palestine. During that era, the Bezalel school influenced a lot of the region's decorative art. This movement, which was something of a combination of Oriental art and European Art Nouveau, flourished during the late Ottoman and British Mandate Periods. Examples of Bezalel art include colorful paintings, often in panels, with Arabic or Hebrew script on them, as well as copperwork, etchings, and wood and ivory carvings.

CHAPTER 6 NORTH AMERICA

North American decorative art has one foot in Native American art and one foot in the cultures that (mostly) European settlers brought to the "New World." Like the people who settled in this rugged country beginning in the sixteenth century, most North American decorative art is less structured, less fussy, and hardier than its European counterparts, and often it incorporates elements of nature into the design, which is typical of Native American design.

For our purposes, we'll define North America as Canada, the United States, and Mexico.

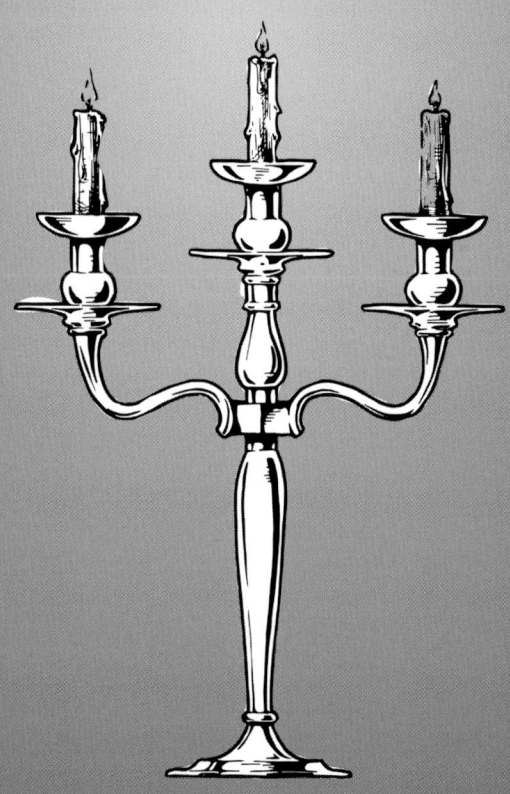

AMERICAN DECORATIVE ART IN THE 17TH AND 18TH CENTURIES

American decorative art in the seventeenth century owes a lot to the European furniture makers, silver- and ironsmiths, and textile weavers of the previous century. Many immigrants from England, France, Germany, and other western European countries brought the skills of the old country with them and gradually adapted them to use the materials of the New World. Thus, seventeenth-century and early eighteenth-century American furniture favors the ornate lines and rich fabrics found in British and French drawing rooms.

Eventually, however, as the colonies became the United States, decorative artists broke away from these fancier styles and created furniture and household

Early American furniture was simple—like this ladderback chair.

The couch in Barack Obama's Green Room of the White House is attributed to furniture craftsman Duncan Phyfe.

items that were simpler, easy to produce, and more utilitarian. For instance, early American tables and chairs have feet and legs that are squared, instead of the carved feet and legs favored in Europe.

Chests became a favorite household item during this period because early European residents of the New World were likely to move on to a new home during their lifetime. Other favorites included ladderback chairs and simple plank farm tables. Most early American furniture was made from the woods that were found locally, such as pine, maple, oak, and cherry.

As Americans got more affluent and became more settled, ornate features began to creep back into American furniture design. The Federalist Period of the late eighteenth century saw the advent of carved legs and finials on furniture, silk upholstery, and less utilitarian pieces, such as dining room sets and grandfather clocks. Popular furniture craftspeople of this period include Duncan Phyfe and Thomas Chippendale.

This is also the period that saw a great expansion of the original United States into the West. By 1821 the original 13 states had turned into a nation of 24 states, and pioneers were traveling by droves to opportunities in the Plains states and the Northwest Territory. Because these pioneers could only take a few of their prized pieces of European-style furniture with them, an entire new style grew up out of necessity. These early pioneer men and women made household goods from what they had on hand, and log beds and plank tables became popular.

AMERICAN DECORATIVE ART IN THE 19TH CENTURY: FORMING A NEW IDENTITY

The nineteenth century saw the United States begin to create its own identity apart from Great Britain and the other European countries whose people populated the towns of the East and, increasingly, the Midwest and Plains states. For those who had the money, Federal-style furniture continued to be all the rage in the early nineteenth century. This was a Neoclassical movement that recalled the days of ancient Greece and Rome. Federal furniture was sleek and regal, with details like eagle medallions, turned chair and cabinet legs, and silk upholstery. This design style lasted until around 1820, when the Empire style popular in Europe began to find its way to the United States.

A sitting room furnished with Federal-style furniture at the Winterthur Museum in Delaware.

The parlor was the central room in Victorian homes.

Empire furniture was also Neoclassical, but it featured more embellishments than Federal pieces, such as scrolls and columns. This design style reflected Napoleon's vision of grandeur and featured asymmetrical "fainting" coaches, elaborate carved cabinets and armoires, and fiddleback chairs. American Empire style remained popular until the mid-nineteenth century.

Until the mid- to late nineteenth century, most American furniture was still handmade. This put beautiful furniture out of the budget of most American families. Mass-production of furniture after the Civil War changed all of that. This Industrial Revolution coincided with the Victorian movement of the late nineteenth and early twentieth centuries and brought elegant dining room sets, parlor sets, and area rugs within the price range of the average middle-class family. Victorian furniture in the United States was formal, opulent, and slightly "over the top." This was the era of the parlor, which was packed with heavy furniture, knickknacks and collections, needlepoint seats, inlaid designs on cabinets, finials atop cabinets, and leaded-glass decorative windows. More expensive woods, such as black walnut, maple, and ash, were commonly used in this period.

MODERN AMERICAN DECORATIVE ART: INSPIRED BY WAR AND PEACE—AND PLASTIC

The twentieth century brought an end to the Victorian Period, as people around the globe eschewed fancy furnishings, clothes, and more for a more streamlined, modern way of life. In the United States, that translated into the Arts and Crafts movement and its simple lines, leather upholstery, built-in cabinets and bookcases, and sparsely furnished rooms.

The Art Deco movement in the United States reflected the optimism and gaiety of the era between the First and Second World Wars. This period saw the completion of some of America's most iconic structures, such as the Empire State Building and Chrysler Building in New York City, the Golden Gate Bridge, and the Hoover Dam, just to name a few. Art Deco is noted for its sleek, rounded lines; its bold geometric shapes; and its lacquered or highly polished wood furniture.

Bakelite, a form of plastic, was introduced in the Art Deco era.

Plastic, in the form of Bakelite, made its first decorative arts appearance during this era, with molded drawer and cabinet pulls, telephones, and lamp shades. Graphic art posters, murals, and art glass were popular accents in this era.

The Art Deco Period ended as the world, and eventually the United States, entered World War II, and manufacturing facilities concentrated on producing war goods rather than furniture and home accessories. At the end of the war, returning veterans wanted something new and different with which to begin their new lives. New suburbs and communities of single-family homes began to sprout up all over the United States. Many of these were ranch-style homes, in sharp contrast to the Arts and Crafts–style and bungalow homes favored by their parents.

Danish Modern–style fixtures were somewhat whimsical.

These new homes were furnished with modular couches, often upholstered in the new plastic Naugahyde covering, Danish Modern–style matched furniture sets with blonde wood and streamlined proportions, and plastic laminate tables. Accents were somewhat whimsical, with *Sputnik*-style lighting fixtures, canvases with splashes of color, fur rugs, and strategically placed wood and rice-paper room dividers.

Louis Comfort Tiffany

One of the most noted designers of the nineteenth century, Louis Comfort Tiffany created intricate stained-glass windows, many of which graced the churches and mansions of the Gilded Age. He also crafted art glass, leaded-glass lamps, and jewelry, and is associated with the Art Nouveau and aesthetic art movements. Tiffany was the first design decorator of Tiffany & Co., the luxury jewelry company founded by his father, Charles Tiffany.

THE INFLUENCE OF CHARLES AND RAY EAMES

Charles and Bernice "Ray" Eames are best known for the famous streamlined lounge chair that bears their surname, examples of which can be found in New York's Museum of Modern Art. However, the Eames's contribution to modern decorative art goes further than just a single chair design. They collaborated on the Eames House, a modern cliffside home in Pacific Palisades, California, that has come to be known as a landmark in twentieth-century architecture, as well as other architectural projects. They were also early adopters of molded plastic and fiberglass in furniture, and they launched a line of colorful textiles that were used by such luminaries as Frank Lloyd Wright in the 1950s.

Charles and Ray Eames are well known for their now-classic furniture designs.

THE ARTS AND CRAFTS MOVEMENT: MAKE IT SIMPLE AND WELL

Popular in the United States between 1880 and 1920, the Arts and Crafts movement was a minimalist response to the fussy and elaborate design of the Victorian era. The hallmarks for this movement were handcrafted furniture and design elements, often including built-in furniture and medieval-themed and folk-style wallpaper and textiles. The ideology of the movement was anti-industrial, with an emphasis on handmade items rather than those that were mass-produced.

Leading designers in this movement include William Morris (who was particularly noted for his hand-stamped wallpaper patterns), Gustav Stickley (noted for the straight-backed chairs that bear his name, and other furniture designs), Frank Lloyd Wright (for architecture), and Ernest Batchelder (for his ceramic tiles). The movement also spawned a number of pottery companies, many of which are still in business today, such as Cincinnati's Rookwood Pottery, Newcomb Pottery in New Orleans, and Teco Pottery in the greater Chicago area. Several utopian communities, including the Byrdcliffe Colony in Woodstock, New York, and Rose Valley in Pennsylvania, grew up as a result of the Arts and Crafts movement.

A vase from the Newcomb Pottery company circa 1902.

CONTEMPORARY MEXICAN DESIGN: COMBINING OLD AND NEW INSPIRATIONS

Modern Mexican contemporary design draws from the country's rich Aztec, Indian, and colonial past, while adding new twists like sleek, angular lines and modern materials. From the colonial era, Mexican furniture favors pine pieces with heavy, cast-iron hardware. From its Aztec heritage, Mexican decorative objects use themes like images of Aztec gods as well as plants and animals.

Mexico's indigenous heritage brings vibrant color to the mix, with bright red, yellow, and orange woven blankets and rugs; colorful wooden masks and figures, especially those that celebrate and honor the "Day of the Dead"; and hand-thrown pottery of every hue. Silverwork and gemstones mined in Mexico, such as opals, amethysts, and malachite, are also often used to embellish decorative items.

Bright colors are used on masks and trinkets that celebrate the Day of the Dead.

ALEUT AND FIRST NATION DESIGN: FORM AND FUNCTION IN A COLD LAND

A traditional Aleut pipe made of ivory and covered in leather.

The native tribes indigenous to the Aleutian Islands of Alaska, known as the Aleut people, are known for their colorful, angular designs and intricate carvings. Decorative art in this region is useful as well as beautiful and includes weaving, weapons, clothing, and masks. Many of these articles are crafted from wood or walrus ivory and adorned with feathers and sea lion whiskers.

The term "First Nation" refers to a variety of indigenous peoples who live above the Arctic Circle in Alaska, Canada, Greenland, and Russia. In Canada, they are the Inuit, and in Alaska, they are the Inupiat tribe. Like the Aleuts, First Nation tribes use materials at hand to make useful objects that just happen to be beautiful. Walrus ivory, seal skin, soapstone, and wood are popular materials in First Nation decorative art, and common items include baskets made from seaweed and coastal grasses, weapons, and cooking vessels. More modern themes include bold block prints of animals and traditional First Nation mythological figures.

AMERICAN ART GLASS: A TRADITION OF PERFECTION

The popular sun glass sculpture by Dale Chihuly.

Louis Comfort Tiffany and his Tiffany Studios weren't the only American creators of spectacular art glass, although they are arguably the best known. Others—such as Steuben Glass Works in Corning, New York; Ohio's Fenton Glass; and Libby Glass in Toledo, Ohio—all contributed to the popularity of high-end art glass in the late nineteenth and early twentieth centuries. In fact, Toledo is known as the "Glass Capital of the World," and the Toledo Museum of Art features an extensive collection of American art glass. More recently, artists such as Dale Chihuly and Harvey Littleton have spearheaded a second American glass art movement.

NORTH AMERICA

NATIVE AMERICAN DESIGN: FUNCTION OVER FORM

Some Native American tribes weave grass, and other materials, into figures.

Native American languages lack a word for art. Although their decorative objects are often wonderfully crafted and unique, Native American cultures often emphasize function over decoration. Thus, a basket may be well-constructed but not "art." Though there are dozens of Native American tribes, each with its own culture and design style, some similarities exist among all or most of the tribes. In addition to stressing function, Native American decorative art makes use of nature, both in its plant and animal themes and in its colors, which are created using berries and other natural dyes. Historically, Native America "artists" used materials found near their homeland: forest tribes carved wood, Plains tribes wove grass, and southwestern tribes molded clay into pottery.

The Shaker style, as seen in this bedroom, was very simple and minimalistic.

SHAKER STYLE: AN EARLY MINIMALIST APPROACH

The United Society of Believers in Christ's Second Appearance (aka the Shakers) were a religious community in the eighteenth, nineteenth, and early twentieth centuries mostly in the Northeast and Midwest. The Shakers were minimalists long before that aesthetic became popular. If a piece of furniture or decorative item didn't also have a use, they didn't want it in their homes. They also shunned ornamentation as prideful and showy. Instead, they used excellent materials, such as fine cherry and oak, as well as the placement of things like drawers to create visual interest. Shaker design is noted for its straight-back chairs (which were designed to hang on pegs on the wall), tall chests of drawers, and long, farmhouse-style tables.

CHAPTER 7 OCEANIA

Oceania is the umbrella name for a vast collection of Pacific islands, as far apart as Hawaii, Samoa, New Zealand, Australia, and Fiji. The people who settled these islands had just one thing in common: their love of the water and the land. Although many islanders had similar ancestors, their individual environments led them to develop new cultures and new art forms.

NATIVE AUSTRALIAN DECORATIVE ART: REMNANTS OF A THREATENED CULTURE

A traditional punu *mask.*

Before the British or the Dutch, before the scores of immigrants arrived from all over the globe, the land that is now Australia was inhabited by a people we call the Aborigines. These people are believed to have first arrived on this land approximately 50,000 years ago. This was a very diverse group, speaking more than 250 different languages. As happened in other parts of the world, diseases brought by Europeans, for which the Aborigines had no immunity, nearly wiped out this civilization of up to 1 million people. Still, many of their crafts and decorative art forms survive today.

Wood carving, weaving, and sand painting were all important art forms in aboriginal culture. Nature and natural themes were prominent in this culture, and the colors red (representing the desert sand), white (the clouds and sky), yellow (the sun), and

Aboriginal basket weavers used to spin human hair into their baskets.

brown (the soil) were most frequently used. As with other early cultures, paintings and designs on clothing and pottery told stories and helped to keep history alive for future generations.

Aboriginal wood carvings, called *punu*, were created using a wire that had been heated in a fire, which was used to burn designs into the wood. Many of these were created in animal shapes and used in tribal ceremonies.

Basket weaving varied among groups, depending on the materials available. Twisted bark fibers were used in the north. Human hair was spun into thread and woven by the tribes of Western Australia, and grasses were combined with hair for weaving by the tribes in the coastal areas, particularly in the south.

COLONIAL INFLUENCE ON AUSTRALIAN DECORATIVE ART

Like Africa, the Caribbean, and Southeast Asia, colonists left their mark on the design history of Australia. The Dutch were the first Europeans to explore Australia, and they called their new settlements New Holland. The British arrived in the late eighteenth century, and immigrants from countries all over the globe followed in the nineteenth and twentieth centuries.

Unlike colonists in other parts of the world, many of the early British settlers arrived with very few possessions, having been banished from England and asked to choose between Australia or prison. For that reason, Australia has a much more frontier style than other colonies. Early settlers brought British

Like other colonial peoples, the Australians put their belongings in wooden chests, except they used gum tree or cedar wood.

Also constructed with Australian woods were four-poster beds.

tastes and design sense with them, but they were forced to create decorative objects from memory using materials at hand—factors that influenced what would become Australian style.

    Much of Australian colonial furniture mirrored the massive British designs of the day, such as four-poster beds and solid sideboards, but they were constructed of Australian woods such as gum tree and cedar. Chests and trunks that had carried immigrants' possessions to their new home were put into use as tables and wardrobes. Sheer fabrics, white walls (often of beadboard), and patterned area rugs over hardwood floors completed the décor.

POLYNESIAN DESIGN: COMMON THEMES IN SEPARATE SOCIETIES

The word "Polynesian" refers to an interconnected group of people who share the same roots. This group includes the native peoples of Tahiti, the Cook Islands, Hawaii, Samoa, and New Zealand. Today, there are still more than 1 million ethnic Polynesians. Inevitably, these groups all created their own individual design styles over the centuries. However, a number of common elements emerge.

- **Water themes:** The Polynesian peoples were all seafarers, and thus they use fish, waves, and other marine motifs to embellish their textiles, pottery, and other decorative items.
- **Tapa cloth:** Although some Polynesian people wove grass into cloth, the majority used bark to make a durable fabric. Most cultures also used wax or batik techniques to create patterns.

Women make kava in the traditional shallow, wooden bowl.

- **Kava bowls**: Kava, a drink with mild sedative and euphoric properties made from the leaves of the kava plant, has been a part of Polynesian culture for centuries. Carved, shallow, wooden bowls designed to hold this beverage are found in most Polynesian societies.
- **Tikis and other statues**: Tikis are best known as a Hawaiian art form. However, these carved, human-like statues of Polynesian gods actually originated with the Maori people of New Zealand. They are found all over the world, and the large stone statues on Easter Island off the coast of Ecuador are thought to be related to the tikis of the South Pacific.
- **Tattoos**: Elaborate tattoos and interlocking decorative designs are another hallmark of Polynesian design. These markings were originally used to express a person's rank, identity, and personality. Nearly all ancient Polynesians had tattoos, often covering their entire body. Eventually, these designs found their way onto textiles, floor coverings, and baskets.

A tiki made of terra-cotta.

Tapa Cloth: Fabric from Trees

Tapa cloth, also known as *kapa*, *siapo*, or *ngato*, is a traditional cloth made from the inner bark of trees and then colored with berries and other natural dyes using stenciling and stamping techniques. Still popular today throughout the South Pacific, from Samoa to Tahiti to the Hawaiian Islands, tapa cloth is used for decorative wall hangings, bedspreads, and ceremonial or wedding garments.

MAORI DESIGN: DISTINCTIVE FORMS FROM A PROUD PEOPLE

The Maori, the first inhabitants of New Zealand, are a Polynesian people who arrived on the islands via canoes and created a unique culture, much of which continues to thrive. Today, there are more than 700,000 native Maori in New Zealand, and many more who have settled other places around the globe.

Although the Maori are perhaps best known for their elaborate tattoos, they are also skilled at many other decorative art forms. These include *whakairo*, a detailed form of carving on bone, stone, and wood; *raranga*, a method of weaving using hand-tying and hand-threading rather than a loom; and *heru*, carved hair ornaments worn by men and women for ceremonies and major life events. Before the arrival of Western settlers, carvings and textiles were used by the Maori to record legends and important tribal stories for future generations.

Whakairo *is a detailed form of carving that the Maori people specialize in.*

Tapa cloth from the eighteenth century.

HAWAIIAN DECORATIVE ART: DISTINCTIVE DESIGNS FROM A NATURAL WONDERLAND

Decorative art in Hawaii, the chain of 137 islands located in the middle of the Pacific Ocean, traditionally makes good use of natural materials such as teakwood, lava, bark cloth, and feathers. Unlike many other cultures, the native Hawaiians didn't produce woven cloth or metalwork. The Hawaiian Islands have had many influences, including Polynesian, Japanese, Chinese, Portuguese and, more recently, American.

    Tapa cloth (*kapa*) adorned most Hawaiian homes, and most properties had a carved tiki statue on hand to protect them. On Maui, where whaling thrived in the nineteenth and early twentieth centuries, intricate ivory carving is still popular. More recently, contemporary decorative artists have flocked to the islands, and ceramics, pottery, and painting have flourished and added to the rich Polynesian heritage in Hawaii.

THE TEXTILES OF NEW GUINEA

New Guinea, the world's second largest island (after Greenland), is located just north of Australia. The eastern half of the island is Papua New Guinea, an independent country since 1975. The western half is called West Papua and is administered by Indonesia. More than 1,000 tribes have called this relatively small island home and, with Dutch, German, and British colonists, forged a unique and singular culture.

The island's textiles provide a perfect example of this New Guinean culture. In addition to tapa cloth—similar to that found in Hawaii, Tonga, Fiji, and other South Pacific islands—New Guinea produces woven cotton fabrics with geometric and striped patterns integrated into them. At one time, each tribe had its own set of designs.

In the late twentieth and early twenty-first centuries, Papua New Guinea has developed a burgeoning fashion industry, with fabrics that combine traditional designs and modern technology.

Traditional handmade Papua New Guinean cloth is hand-painted with natural dyes using geometric patterns.

A woman sits and creates a quilt using the tivaevae technique.

TIVAEVAE, THE TRADITIONAL ART OF QUILTING IN THE COOK ISLANDS

Tivaevae is a form of quilting unique to the Cook Islands. Located in the middle of the South Pacific, the Cook Islands are a collection of 15 islands and are now a part of New Zealand. Women on these islands practice *tivaevae*, an elaborate form of hand-quilting. They create large, colorful bed coverings and tapestries, many of which are handed down from generation to generation. Most likely introduced to the islands by Christian missionaries, *tivaevae* has become an important social activity, with many sewers often working on the same piece. Though the needlework technique may be European, the patterns of colorful flowers, animals, and fish are decidedly Polynesian.

FIJIAN WOOD CARVING: DRUMS, MASKS, AND TURTLES

Fiji is well known around the world for its beautiful carved wooden objects. Considered a "male" craft on this Pacific island, the men of Fiji have produced a variety of decorative, combat, and household items for centuries, including clubs and spear handles, drum bases, ceremonial masks, and tanoa drinking bowls, used for serving Fiji's national drink, kava. Fijian carvers traditionally used native vesi wood, but they have largely switched to sandalwood, which is more sustainable. Many Fijian wood carvings feature an image of a sea turtle, a recurrent symbol in Fiji lore.

A man drinks kava out of a tanoa drinking bowl.

LAPITA POTTERY: A RARE ART FORM IN THE REGION

Unlike most parts of the globe, the peoples of Polynesia and Oceania do not have an early history of pottery making. This has to do with the materials available to early island inhabitants. Most had sand and lava, rather than clay, to work with. One notable exception to this rule is Lapita pottery. Found in archaeological sites in the Western Pacific region and New Guinea, this brown and white, low-fired pottery bears intricate designs and frequently a dental (toothed) stamp. The Lupita people are thought to have come from Southeast Asia, settling in what is now Melanesia.

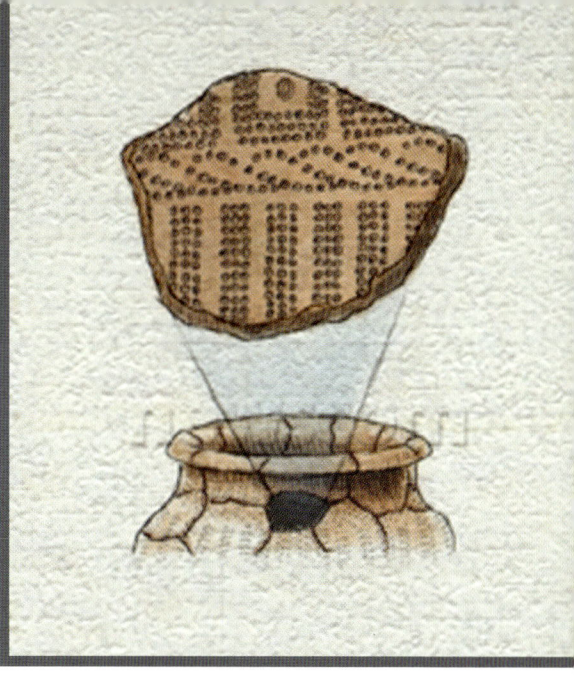

This illustration depicts what the dental stamp looks like on Lapita pottery.

VICTORIAN DECORATIVE ART IN AUSTRALIA

Decorative art in Australia has a strong British influence, and, although it is a sovereign, independent nation, this country remains strongly tied to the United Kingdom. Settlers from Great Britain began arriving in the last part of the eighteenth century, and immigration escalated in the nineteenth century, just as the Victorian age was blossoming in England. For this reason, much of eastern Australia's early colonial architecture and furnishings bore the distinct, elaborate, dark, and fancy mark of Victorian design. However, because materials and climate in this part of the world were decidedly different from those of England, adaptations had to be made, such as using native jarrah and gumwood rather than British oak and maple.

Flinders Street Station in Melbourne is a perfect example of the lingering Victorian design.

FURTHER READING & INTERNET RESOURCES

BOOKS

Bloom, Jonathan, and Sheila Blair. *Islamic Arts*. London: Phaidon Press, 1997.
Campbell, Gordan (Ed.). *The Grove Encyclopedia of Decorative Arts*. Oxford, UK: Oxford University Press, 2006.
Honour, Hugh, and John Fleming. *A World History of Art*. London: Macmillan, 1982.
Kirkham, Pat, Susan Weber, and the Bard Graduate Center. *History of Design: Decorative Arts and Material Culture, 1400–2000*. New Haven, CT: Yale University Press, 2013.
Spring, Chris. *African Textiles Today*. Washington, DC: Smithsonian Books, 2012.

WEB SITES

www.kenya-information-guide.com/maasai-tribe.html. The arts and crafts of the Maasai.
https://lanka.com/about/interests/handicrafts/. The handicraft traditions of Sri Lanka.
www.thoughtco.com/lost-treasure-of-the-inca-2136548. The story of the lost treasure of the Incas.
www.gounesco.com/guatemalas-beautiful-vibrant-textiles/. An exploration of the textiles of Guatemala.
https://www.metmuseum.org/toah/hd/cali/hd_cali.htm. "Calligraphy in Islamic Art" by the Metropolitan Museum of Art's Department of Islamic Art.
researcharchive.calacademy.org/research/anthropology/persia/history.htm. "The History of Persian Ceramics" from the California Academy of Sciences.
https://artgallery.yale.edu/american-decorative-arts. The Yale Art Gallery's collection of American decorative arts.
https://study.com/academy/lesson/19th-century-american-furniture-history-designers-styles.html. The history, designers, and styles of nineteenth-century American furniture.
www.kapahawaii.com/. Site devoted to the preservation of the art of Hawaiian kapa, or bark cloth making.
www.go-fiji.com/artsandcrafts.html. A survey of Fiji's arts and crafts.

INDEX

Aboriginal art forms, 82–83
Adam style (Europe), 44
African contemporary design, 18
African religions, influence of, 20
African textiles, 12–13, 18–19
Aleut and First Nation tribes, 79
American glass art, 75, 79
Andes Mountains, art forms of, 53, 56
arabesque design, 67
Art Deco, 41, 74–75
Arts and Crafts Movement, 39, 74, 77
Australian style, 84–85, 93

basket weaving, 80, 83
bowls, 31, 53, 87, 92
British influences, 10–11, 37, 38–39, 40, 44, 84–85, 93
Buddhist art, 28
Byzantine design, 60–61

calligraphy, 58, 63
Cambodia, 29
carving, 17, 54, 55, 56, 83, 87, 88, 92
cassoni (marriage chests), 43
ceramics, 25, 32, 48, 67
China, 22–23, 31, 32
colonial influences, 9–11, 48–49, 84–85

Danish Modern design, 42, 75
designers, 33, 39, 41, 75, 76, 77

Eames, Charles and Bernice "Ray," 76
Egypt, 14–15
Egyptian Revival, 15, 44
18th-century European design, 36–37
European design styles, 36–42, 44
European influences, 9–11, 48–49, 69–72, 84, 90, 93

fabric. *see* textiles
family crests, 43
Fijian wood carving, 92

furniture, 10–11, 36–37, 42, 56, 61, 70–78, 80, 85

glass art, 68, 75, 79
gods and goddesses, 14, 23, 30, 47, 53, 87
Guatemala, 54

Haiti, 55
Hawaii, 89
Hindu art, 30

Inca Empire, 47, 52
Indian subcontinent, 26–27
Islam, art of, 58–59, 63, 64
Islamic glass, 68
Israel, 62–63, 68

jade, use of, 32
Jamaica, 50–51, 56
Japan, 24–25, 27, 31
Japanese panels, 27

lacquerware, 31
Lapita pottery, 93
Latin American art forms, 50–51, 55

Maasai tribe, 15, 16
Māori art forms, 87, 88
masks, 20, 82
metalwork, 26–27, 52, 59
Mexico, contemporary, 78
Middle Eastern art renaissance, 62–63
Modern American styles, 74–75, 76
mosaics, 48, 60, 67

Native American design, 80
neoclassical style, 37, 44, 72–73
Nepal, 31
New Guinean textiles, 90
19th-century American styles, 72–73
19th-century European design, 38–39

origami, 24
Ottoman Empire, legacy of, 64

Persian rugs and pottery, 65, 66
Polynesian design, 86–87
porcelain, fine, 22, 32
pottery, 25, 32, 50, 66, 77, 93
pre-Columbian art forms, 46–47, 56

quilting, 91

raffia cloth, 19
religions, influences of, 20, 28, 30, 34–35, 49, 51, 55, 58–61, 68, 80
Renaissance Europe, 34–35
rugs (Middle East), 57, 59, 65

sculpture, 17, 22, 51, 79
17th and 18th centuries American styles, 70–71
Shaker style, 80
silk weaving, 29
South American silver, 53
Spanish colonial influences, 48–49, 55
statues, 14, 28, 47, 49, 55, 87, 89
symbols, 23, 28, 30, 92

tapa cloth, 86, 87, 89, 90
textiles, 12–13, 18–19, 26, 29, 54, 56, 87, 90
Tiffany, Louis Comfort, 75, 79
tiles, ceramic, 48, 67
tivaevae quilting (Cook Islands), 91
tribal art, 15–17, 46–47, 51, 79, 80

United States, design styles of, 70–75

Vatican City, Rome, 35
Victorian design, 39, 40, 73, 93

weaponry, 16, 92
wood carving, 17, 54, 55, 56, 83, 87, 88, 92

Yoruba textiles, 12, 19

AUTHOR'S BIOGRAPHY

Sandy Mitchell Pavick is a full-time freelance writer and former interior designer. She is also the author of two books on Cleveland history, *Cleveland's Little Italy* and *Cleveland's Slavic Village*. She has restored and decorated two antique homes and is currently working with her husband on converting a cabin in the woods into her dream home for the two of them, their dog, and three cats.

CREDITS

COVER

(clockwise from top left) jade lion, Vietnam, Gooddenka/iStock; Tilework at Shah Mosque, Isfahan, Iran, guenterguni/iStock; Peruvian textiles, Denis Mantilla/Dreamstime; Barcelona chairs by Ludwig Mies van de Rohe and Lilly Reich, Ragoarts/Dreamstime; Art Nouveau subway sign by Hector Guimard, Paris, France, dennisvdw/iStock; Australian aboriginal didgeridoos, lore/iStock

INTERIOR

1, Kouze59/Shutterstock; 2–3, Vrakis/Dreamstime; 5, Dmitry Rukhlenko/Shutterstock; 7, (clockwise from top left) Gooddenka/iStock, lore/iStock, Ragoarts/Dreamstime, Denis Mantilla/Dreamstime, dennisvdw/iStock, guenterguni/iStock; 9, NGvozdeva/iStock; 10, Svitlana Belinska/Dreamstime; 11, Anton Starikov/Dreamstime; 12, Yaayi/Shutterstock; 13, Anina Lonte/Shutterstock; 14, mountainpix/Shutterstock; 15, Africa Studio/Shutterstock; 16, A. Davey/Wikimedia Commons; 17, Rixie/Dreamstime; 18, Tinasdreamworld/Dreamstime; 19, (UP) Cliff/Wikimedia Commons; 19, (LO) Werner Forman Archive Heritage Images/Newscom; 20, (UP) Africanway/iStock; 20, (LO) Goddard_Photography/iStock; 21, Godruma/Dreamstime; 22, Alison Henley/Shutterstock; 23, New Africa/Shutterstock; 24, Eiko Tsuchiya/Shutterstock; 25, Anirut Thailand/Shutterstock; 26, Izanbar/Dreamstime; 27, Stbernardstudio/Dreamstime; 28, Luke SW/Shutterstock; 29, JoanneJean/Shutterstock; 30, I love photo/Shutterstock; 31, (UP) Zoran Karapancev/Shutterstock; 31, (LO) Dmitry Chulov/Shutterstock; 32, (UP) Nantarpat Surasingthothong/Dreamstime; 32, (LO) Lei Xu/Dreamstime; 33, Ina Graur Frimu/Dreamstime; 34, S-F/Shutterstock; 35, MACH Photos/Shutterstock; 36, Anastasiia Guseva/Dreamstime; 37, Honzik7/Dreamstime; 38, IR Stone/Shutterstock; 39, William Morris/Wikimedia Commons; 40, Anton_Ivanov/Shutterstock; 41, Coralimages2020/Dreamstime; 42, olgagorovenko/Shutterstock; 43, (UP) Luis Garcia/Wikimedia Commons; 43, (LO) Klodien/Dreamstime; 44, (UP) Wikimedia Commons; 44, (LO) Vvoevale/Dreamstime; 45, Prokhorovich/Shutterstock; 46, Anna Sulencka2/Shutterstock; 47, W. Scott McGill/Shutterstock; 48, Radiokafka/Dreamstime; 49, Mminnano/Shutterstock; 50, Guillermo Arévalo Aucahuasi/Wikimedia Commons; 51, SL-Photography/Shutterstock; 52, Watch The World/Shutterstock; 53, Werner Forman Archive Heritage Images/Newscom; 54, bumhills/Shutterstock; 55, (UP) Markpittimages/Dreamstime; 55, (LO) arindambanerjee/Shutterstock; 56, (UP) Debbie Ann Powell/Shutterstock; 56, (LO) Pixattitude/Dreamstime; 57, Apanggeleng/Dreamstime; 58, mrfiza/Shutterstock; 59, Elena Zhi/Shutterstock; 60, Artur Bogacki/iStock; 61, akg-images/Newscom; 62, delihavat/iStock; 63, Fotokon/Dreamstime; 64, isa_ozdere/iStock; 65, efesenko/iStock; 66, Marie-Lan Nguyen/Wikimedia Commons; 67, (UP) ColorMaker/Shutterstock; 67, (LO) Jan Smith/Wikimedia Commons; 68, (UP) Daderot/Wikimedia Commons; 68, (LO) K45025/Dreamstime; 69, Alexander Babich/Dreamstime; 70, Milesbeforeisleep/Shutterstock; 71, Pete Souza/Wikimedia Commons; 72, Daderot/Wikimedia Commons; 73, EPG_EuroPhotoGraphics/Shutterstock; 74, Antonio Gravante/Dreamstime; 75, Poul Henningsen/Wikimedia Commons; 76, Pablo Scapinachis/Dreamstime; 77, Newcomb Pottery, Brooklyn Museum/Wikimedia Commons; 78, Legacy1995/Dreamstime; 79, (UP) Ken Backer/Dreamstime; 79, (LO) Anne Richard/Dreamstime; 80, (UP) Anna Krivitskaia/Dreamstime; 80, (LO) Doug Coldwell/Wikimedia Commons; 81, Aratehortua/Dreamstime; 82, VisFineArt/Shutterstock; 83, Wiritjiribin/Dreamstime; 84, Nylakatara2013/Dreamstime; 85, Steveheap/Dreamstime; 86, Gerd Kohlmus/Dreamstime; 87, Eddydegroot/Dreamstime; 88, robert cicchetti/Shutterstock; 89, Wmpearl/Wikimedia Commons; 90, Danita Delmont/Shutterstock; 91, John Colles Burland/Wikimedia Commons; 92, Eliaviel/Dreamstime; 93, (UP) QAI Publishing Universal Images Group/Newscom; 93, (LO) Benjawan Sittidech/Dreamstime